P9-AQE-459

Reader Phillips
Phillips, Joan.
Walt Disney's Mickey Mouse
and the pet show

MAY 21 '90

DATE DUE

Walt Disney's

Mickey Mouse
and the Pet Show

Walt Disney's
Mickey Mouse and the Pet Show

By Joan Phillips
Illustrated by Darrell Baker

A Golden Book • New York
Western Publishing Company, Inc., Racine, Wisconsin 53404

Mickey Mouse and Donald Duck
were taking a walk.
Pluto was with them.

They saw a man
putting up a sign.
The sign said,
"Bring your pet
to pet show today!"

"Pluto can be in the pet show!"
said Mickey.
"Yes," said Donald.
"But he needs a bath."

Pluto heard the word *bath*.
Pluto knew the word *bath*.
Pluto did not want a bath!
Pluto ran away.

Mickey ran after Pluto.
Donald ran after Mickey.
They ran up a street.

Pluto could not run away.
They all went to Mickey's house.

Mickey got out the tub.
Minnie put in the water.

Daisy got out the towels.
Goofy put in the soap.
Everything was ready.
But where was Pluto?

Everyone looked for Pluto.
They looked for a long time.
They could not find him.

"I am tired," said Mickey.
"I am going to sit down."

Mickey sat down.
"Bow-wow!" said the chair.
It was Pluto!

"Come on, Pluto.
You must have a bath!"
said Mickey.
Mickey put Pluto into the tub.

Pluto got all wet.
Mickey got all wet, too.
So did Minnie and Goofy
and Donald and Daisy!

Mickey washed Pluto with soap.
The soap made Pluto slide.

Pluto slid out of Mickey's hands.
He tried to run away again.

"Pluto, stop!
Do not go in my car!"
cried Mickey.
But Pluto jumped into the car.

Mickey ran to the car.
Pluto jumped out of the car.

Pluto saw Mickey's face.
He did not see
where he was going.

He did not see
the clothesline.
Crash!

"Come on, Pluto.
You must have a bath!"
said Mickey.

Oh, no!
Look at Mickey and Pluto!

Mickey put Pluto back
into the tub.
"Do not run away again!"
said Mickey.
"You must have a bath!"

Pluto knew he had to
have a bath.
He did not try
to run away again.
But he sang.

At last Pluto was ready.
"Put a bow on him,"
said Daisy.

Pluto did not want a bow.
"Hold on to him!"
cried Mickey.
"Hold on to him!"
cried Donald and Daisy.
"Put the bow on him!"
cried Goofy and Minnie.

Oh, no!
Look at Donald!

At last Pluto was ready.
He looked great!
Everyone walked to
the pet show.

They all saw the sign.
They saw *all* of the sign.
The sign said, "Bring your pet *cat*
to pet show today!"

"Pluto is not a *cat*!"
said Mickey.
"Pluto is a dog!
He can not be in
the pet show!"

But Pluto did not care.
He looked great!
He felt great!
He would not need
another bath
for a very long time!